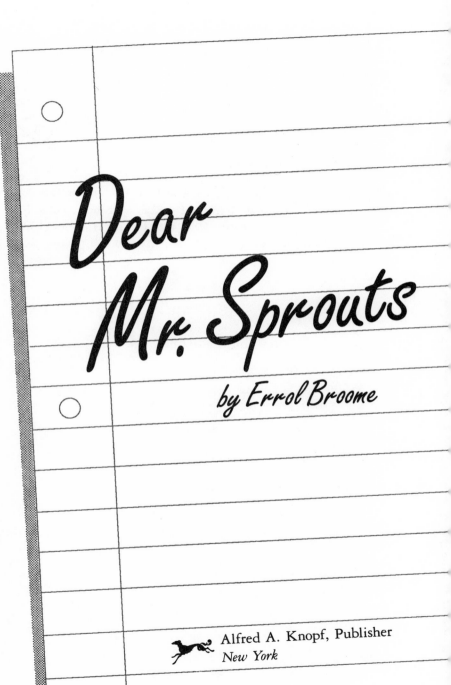

Dear
Mr. Sprouts

by Errol Broome

Alfred A. Knopf, Publisher
New York

Special thanks to John Fisher and staff of the Speech Pathology Department of the Royal Children's Hospital, Melbourne, and to Nan Oates, whose story "Putting the Heart Back into the Heartbreak Hills," *(Trees and Natural Resources,* vol. 28, no. 4, 1986), was the inspiration for this book.

THIS IS A BORZOI BOOK PUBLISHED BY ALFRED A. KNOPF, INC.

Library of Congress Cataloging-in-Publication Data
Broome, Errol.
  Dear Mr. Sprouts / by Errol Broome.
     p.   cm.
  Summary: As Freddie's seeds grow in the Australian bush, so does his friendship with a secretive pen pal.
  ISBN 0-679-83714-0 (trade)
  [1. Letters—Fiction. 2. Pen pals—Fiction. 3. Trees—Fiction. 4. Australia—Fiction.]   I. Title.
PZ7.B79945De   1993
[Fic]—dc20   92-13490

Manufactured in the United States of America
10 9 8 7 6 5 4 3 2 1

For people like the McCubbins,
who did this in the Strzeleckis

Dear American Reader,

G'day! Anke and I are a bit stumped by all this. We never thought you'd be reading our stuff. "Read those letters?" I said to her. "It was bad enough writing them!"

Out here, we think you Yanks have a funny way of talking. In case you think *we* have a funny way of talking, here are some words and expressions you need to know.

Good luck there,

Freddie

"a bit jack of the place" — "a little fed up with the place"
"all over his dial" — "all over his face"
"as if I had a roo loose in the top paddock" — "as if I were nuts" (roo=kangaroo)
"Azif!" — "Not likely!" (a contraction of "As if!")
backblocks — the remote parts of the country: the boonies; the sticks
biscuits — cookies
bitumen — asphalt
bogan — a very uncool person: nerd
boot — the trunk of a car

bush sense—rural "street smarts"

"by yonks"—"a long time"

caravan—a van or trailer used for recreational camping

carpark—a parking lot

"Everything's jake"—"Everything's okay"

footie—Australian Rules football

"Have a cuppa"—"Have a cup of tea, coffee, etc."

"I must have cheesed him off"—"I must have irritated him"

jigged about—danced around

jumper—a sweater

"like a nutter"—"like a crazy person"

on the dole—receiving money from the government, as a welfare or unemployment benefit

paddock—pastureland, usually fenced in

pinnies—pinball

posh—smart, swanky

road box—a rural mailbox

ute—a pickup truck

Vegemite—a brand of black, sticky vegetable sandwich spread

wardrobe—a closet

"when I had a needle"—"when I got a shot" (from a doctor)

willy-willy—a small, severe whirling windstorm

wombat—a bearlike animal that has a pouch and sleeps underground

12 April 1983

Anke was nine when she let the balloon go.

The schoolyard was a forest of green balloons, each with an envelope of seed attached. Anke gripped the end of the string and read the name on the envelope:

Eucalyptus regnans *(Mountain ash)*

She did not know what this seed might grow into, but it sounded taller than anything she had ever seen.

"One, two, three—GO!" called Miss Munns. Anke let go of the string. Everybody set their balloons free. They rose in a cloud above the roof, over the bitumen yard, past the corner shop and the car park, up, up, bobbing and spinning on waves of air. They left the busy streets behind and spilled in different directions across the suburbs, over the hills, away into places where Anke had never been.

*　　　*　　　*

"Look!" said Freddie.

Dad looked across the scrub, over the dead hills to the sky. He saw a bright dot blowing towards the creek. "What's a balloon doing out here? Nobody's had a birthday."

Freddie jumped from the tank-stand and ran across the

yard. His gumboots slipped in the mud. "Come on, Dad," he yelled. "It's coming down. Let's get it."

"I'll be buggered!" Dad stared at the envelope in his hand. "This thing's come all the way from Middleton."

"Where's that?"

"In the city."

"That's 151 kilometers!" One thing Freddie knew, Weatherly was 151 kilometers from the city. It wasn't far in a fast car, but when you lived out here, alone with your father, and the mud sucked at your boots while the weeds tore your heart out, when you struggled with all that, you didn't often get to the city.

"What else does it say, Dad?"

"Here, read it yourself."

Freddie sat on the edge of an iron trough that brimmed with pea-green water. "It's got seeds," he said. "Shit! They want us to plant them. And then we're meant to write to this person and tell them."

"Then we will," said Dad. "You can do it, OK?"

"Me? I'm not planting seeds. I'm not writing letters, either."

"Oh, come on, Freddie. Give us a break. You can do it while I get at the bracken."

Freddie grunted. "I always have to do everything." He put the seeds in his pocket and dragged the limp balloon behind him as he trudged across the paddock. "They'll never grow . . . and where are we going to plant them?"

Dad scanned the dark hills and shrugged. *"We'll try the hills. We could do with some trees up there."* Under his breath he muttered: *"Reckon they could've sent us something more useful than a few lousy seeds."*

23 April 1983

Dear Anke,
Thank you for the seeds. We found them on Wednesday. I planted them in old trays from the shed but ants got some. My Dad says it's funny you sent mountain ash, because they used to grow here before we came.

Yours faithfully,

Frederick Forth

18 May 1983

Dear Frederick,
Thank you for your letter. Miss Munns, my teacher, is pleased you found the seeds. We hope your trees grow.

Yours sincerely,

Anke Duyker

Year 4

31 May 1983

Dear Anke,
Dad says to tell you the seeds have sprouted. They look like hairs on a dog's back. He says *I* have to look after them.

Yours faithfully,

Frederick Forth

21 July 1983

Dear Frederick,
My friend Dee did not get a letter. Only seven people in my year got letters. Miss Munns wants to know what happened to the trees that grew on your farm before, and what grows there now. What year are you in at school?

From

Anke Duyker

17 September 1983

Dear Anke,
Before we came, people chopped down the trees to make farms. But it's no good farming here. We get mud in winter and fires in summer. We get weeds—bracken and ragwort and blackberries. They scratch my legs. I've got cuts all over me.

Yours faithfully,

Frederick Forth

19 October 1983

Dear Frederick,
Thank you for your letter. What I want to know is why do you stay there if it is so bad? And how are your sprouts?

From

Anke Duyker

16 November 1983

Dear Anke,
Nobody will buy this place and we've got nowhere else
to go. The trees are coming on OK. They're in tubes
now—hundreds of them—but some died. I never stop
looking after them.

Yours faithfully,

Freddie

14 December 1983

Dear Frederick,
This is to say Happy Christmas. Miss Munns hopes
you will tell us about the trees next year too. Have
you got a Christmas tree?

From

Anke

21 January 1984

Dear Anke,
Your letter made Dad remember the tree Gran sent six years ago. He forgot it when Mum shot through to Darwin. It's made of foil and your teeth hurt if you bite it. Dad found it in the shed and he made me put it together. Gran came from Sale for Christmas, so I had to sleep on the verandah with the spiders.

From

Freddie

4 March 1984

Dear Frederick,
I'm glad you found the tree in the shed. This time
Mammie bought a tree in a pot, like the ones that
grow in the Netherlands only smaller. I made a star
for the tree, but I left it at school. Beatrix—she's
my sister only she's moved out—brought home special things from the shop where she works. They
made the tree look nice. I wish we had lots of people
to see it. My friend Dee had a tree with lights. What
I want to know is, why you want to bite the Christmas tree?

Love from
Anke

9 October 1984

Dear Frederick,
I did not get an answer to my letter. I hope you are well. Two weeks ago it was my birthday. I did not have a party. We went to McDonald's with Beatrix. They made me order for everyone. I hate ordering. But it was my birthday and I got an extra-thick shake. Pappie keeps asking about "de boomen." That's what he calls your trees. My teacher wants to know too. What else do you grow on your farm? And you never told me what year you are in.

Love from

Anke

8 December 1984

Dear Anke,

I could go for a Big Mac. Sorry I don't write much, but these trees take time. Dad and I planted them out on the western hill. There were about 926, but sometimes we lost count.

It's rained all year and the place is a mudheap. Dad says wait till next year and the loan will come through. Then he can get a new tractor and plow up the weeds and put in pasture and things. I bet he makes me do half of it. We've got rabbits too.

From

Freddie

17 December 1984

Dear Freddie,
Have you got any other pets? Dee has a cocker span-
iel called Joe but it's really her gran's. Dee lives with
her gran around the corner. I go there sometimes.
Dee is my best friend since Beatrix left. I'm glad
Beatrix doesn't go to university. She comes home
sometimes and brings things from work like china
dogs and photo frames. Beatrix would be a terrible
doctor, anyway. She fainted when I had a needle. I
don't want to be a doctor, either, but don't tell anyone.

Love from
Anke

28 January 1985

Dear Anke,

Rabbits aren't pets. Not at our place, anyhow. What I need is a dog, because there's not much else doing around here. We've got no shops or movies except at Bundaree.

I don't think much about what I'll do one day, but I'd be one brick short of a load if I hung around this place.

From

Freddie

15 February 1985

Dear Freddie,

Today we've been in Australia for ten years. Dee came around with a Dutch cake her gran had made for us. Pappie said "vot's dat?" He says "vot's dat" to everything, especially when he's trying to get Mammie to talk English. Beatrix was coming after work, but she went to a gig with her boyfriend instead. Mammie says now it's up to me. I wish she didn't say that all the time.

After Dee had gone, Pappie said he'd never seen a cake like that in Holland. We ate it all, anyhow.

Love from

Anke

5 March 1985

Dear Anke,
Yesterday Miss Ritter made us write about trees. I couldn't think of a thing. I hate school. Miss Ritter goes: "Frederick, I thought you were growing trees." And I go: "That doesn't mean I can write about them." And she goes: "Stay in at lunchtime and do it then." I go: "I'd rather not, thanks all the same." She gets all red and blown-up like a football and yells: "You'll do what I say," so bang goes my lunchtime. I hate the classroom at lunchtime, because that's when you notice the smells like little kids have peed their pants. Each day I can hardly wait to get out of the place. But then the little kids get on the bus after school and I don't get away from the stink until the 25 kilometer peg. I don't know what people think is so good about the country.

From

Freddie

31 March 1985

Dear Freddie,

At our school we aren't all mixed up in ages like you are. I have lots of people in my class, but Dee is my friend. We collect photos of film stars. Dee wrote to Mel Gibson and got an autographed photo. I was going to write to Sam Neill, but I forgot. I like his voice, so I'm going to write tonight. Do you collect anything? And another thing I want to know is what *do* you like?

Love from

Anke

18 April 1985

Dear Anke,
Some things I might like are:
1. Seeing Geelong vs. Collingwood
2. A trail bike
3. McDonald's
4. Living somewhere else.

Love
Freddie

12 May 1985

Dear Freddie,
Pappie says most people want to live somewhere else
sometimes. Mammie does, but she doesn't say so.
Pappie just knows. He told me that one day he'll
take Mammie back to see her sister, but he hasn't
told Mammie. He pretends he doesn't know. If he
tells her enough that she likes it here, he hopes that
in time she will. Perhaps you could try this too.

Love from
Anke

3 August 1985

Dear Freddie,
You didn't answer my last letter. I want to know, did the loan ever arrive? If it did, and it's a good one, maybe you won't get cut legs again.

We had Open Day at my school at the end of term and it was horrible. I told Mammie not to talk to my friends, but she never stopped. Her English was terrible. Pappie just laughs all the time. I don't know how everyone in the world ended up talking so many different languages when there are only so many sounds you can make when you open your mouth. It makes things *so* complicated.

Last night was good because I slept at Dee's place. She has a room upstairs with two beds and her own television. It's the first time I've slept at someone else's house. Dee's gran cooked lasagna and we didn't get to sleep until nearly morning. Dee and I have made a pact to be friends for life.

Love from
Anke

6 October 1985

Dear Anke,
The loan came. It isn't a thing you really see. Dad heard
about it one afternoon, then he bought a tractor and
started plowing up the weeds in the home paddock. He
goes all day and half the night and is pretty buggered
by the end of the day.

Something else happened too. A logger ran over a
wombat. Dad was coming home from Bundy and he
saw it. The truck didn't even stop. So what do you
know—Dad comes home with this baby wombat! He
reckons he couldn't leave it behind. It was standing in
the middle of the road beside the mother when Dad
got out of the ute. He moved the body to the edge of
the road, but the baby kept on hanging around. It's *really*
cute. Dad thinks so too.

First we got the wildlife people to say OK, we can
keep it for a while. Then we got all these instructions,
like a kilometer long, telling us what to do. I told Dad,
I always wanted a dog and what do I get—a wombat.
He says he always wanted a wombat!

First night he pooped inside the saucepan cupboard.
Then he started gnawing a leg of the table. Dad went
outside and brought in a great log and dumped it in the
middle of the kitchen. "Cut your teeth on that, Digger,"
he said.

We haven't had much sleep since Digger came to stay. He crashes around the house all night. Dad reckons he's fresh out of the pouch, poor little bugger.

Love

Freddie

14 December 1985

Dear Freddie,
I've never seen a wombat, except in the zoo. Please keep on telling me about Digger. Christmas comes soon, and ours will be good this year, because Mammie has said Beatrix can bring her boyfriend. His name is Whizz. Pappie calls him Gee when Beatrix isn't here. Mammie is unhappy, because Whizz doesn't work. He makes good jewelry, though. And he acted in a play once. The other day I told Mammie her English was getting better. She pretended she didn't care, but she was pleased, really.

Happy Christmas, with love from

Anke

4 February 1986

Dear Anke,

Digger has grown heaps. He followed me around all holidays. Dad reckons he's about 12 months old now. We made him a bed in my wardrobe. When I took him for a walk last week, he dug a great hole under the house. Dad said: "Hell's teeth, Freddie, the house will fall down if you don't watch that animal." Then he takes Digger on his knees and talks to him like he's a baby, while guess-who mixes the milk and unblocks the teat and all that. Digger wants to play all night, so sometimes he sleeps on my bed. (Don't tell Dad this: he sleeps *in* the bed. A fellow needs a burrow, doesn't he?)

While all this is happening, the trees keep growing too and now they're bigger than me. Dad says why don't I plant more, so one day there could be a forest here like before. He must have rocks in his head.

Love

Freddie

14 March 1986

Dear Freddie,
I want to tell you about our Christmas. Whizz was fun—except I forgot to buy him a present. He wore a sort of clown's suit and his hair stuck up in orange spikes. I thought Mammie would pass out when they came to the door. But when he opened his mouth, he had this velvet voice like a hypnotist. I just liked listening to him talk. Pretty soon, Mammie started smiling too.

After lunch, Whizz acted like Santa Claus in his clown suit, only this was his real gear, I think. And he'd made these great rings for Mammie and me when he didn't even know us, as well as a bracelet for Beatrix. When he left, he called me Little Sister.

He and Beatrix don't come around much and when they do Mammie makes sure Dee has gone home. I want Dee to meet him. Dee is my only friend who listens.

Mammie works near a place where you buy native seeds, so here are some more in case you want to start your forest. Only one thing bothers me—do wombats eat seedlings?

Love from

Anke

12 May 1986

Dear Anke,
I've got rocks in my head too. I planted your new seed.
Someone said to put the trays on wet newspaper and
it's a whole lot better than drowning them from the top.
I don't reckon Digger will eat the seedlings. He eats
more grass now and he's a sucker for chocolate biscuits. Dad says: "Freddie, you'll ruin him," and then I
catch him feeding Digger toast and honey.

When he wants to play—Digger that is—he butts me
in the legs. Got no manners, that wombat. He comes
to life around dinner time each night—hides behind the
door and jumps out at me. I have to chase him around
the kitchen table and, if I stop, he starts chasing me!
The rest of the time, he's sort of goofy. Snuffling goofy.
I'm getting him used to the bush outside. We go for
walks in the afternoon—me and my wombat. He gets
digging practice, but he never lets me out of his sight.
I reckon a wombat could be a friend for life.

Love

Freddie

9 June 1986

Dear Freddie,

At school today we had to give talks in class. I said
I'd talk on forests. I had it all worked out. I was
going to tell them about your trees and how they
grew half a meter the first year and all that. I made
it like a story and it felt good. Then, when they
started the talks, I felt terrible. I hid behind Richard Stinson in front of me, so Mr. Dunne wouldn't
pick me. The bell rang before my turn, so I got out
of it. Afterwards, Dee said mine would have been
the best.

How is Digger, and do you really think you could
have a forest again?

Love from

Anke

7 August 1986

Dear Anke,

Don't talk about forests. I've got rows of trees in tubes.
I start counting, and I get nearly to the end of a row
then I forget. Dad says there are thousands. Some ani-

mal—not Digger—knocked a whole lot over, so I built a kind of fence. Then junk blew in and smothered a few hundred. Bugs ate a few hundred more. Sometimes I wish a flood would come and wash away the whole bloody lot.

If it wasn't for Digger, I might not have hung around so long. Trouble is, he likes me. But soon he's got to go. Now he wants to come everywhere in the ute with us. We took him shopping the other day. He came to Bundy with Dad and me, sitting on my knee and talking all the time. At the hotel it said NO DOGS, so Dad said: "You can't bring Digger in here." "It doesn't say NO WOMBATS," I said. He said: "It doesn't say NO ELEPHANTS either, but you wouldn't bring one in, would you?" So I sat in the ute with Digger and Dad brought us out a lemonade.

We've worked out Digger is about 18 months old now. Last Thursday I lost him for about half an hour. He turned up with muddy claws and a shy look, like he felt guilty about something. I reckon he's dug himself a good burrow somewhere out there.

Love

Freddie

26 September 1986

Dear Freddie,

Yesterday was my thirteenth birthday. Pappie brought me six yellow tulips. Mammie cried when she saw them, so I hid them behind books on my shelf. I felt terrible. Pappie came and said Mammie was not crying because she didn't like tulips, she was crying because they made her think of home. He told her: "In Holland I do know there is not today a tulip to be seen. But here, we have tulips in Australia in September!" Pappie always thinks of the good things. He says that when I'm sixteen, we'll go back to The Netherlands to see our cousins. It would be nice to have friends like that. Pappie keeps saying: "Anke, we will do dat."

Now the tulips are on the table, where everybody can see them.

Love from

Anke

P.S. Another thing I forgot to tell you—our hockey team did not lose a match.

3 November 1986

Dear Anke,
You have a bloody good time up there—hockey and who knows what. Here, we only get teams for special days. If I lived in the city, I'd play sport every day. You can do anything you like in the city. And do you know what I do? I watch trees grow, and a wombat pretending he's my brother.

Love

Freddie

4 December 1986

Dear Freddie,
I'd like to be good at hockey, but I'm not, so there.
I'm just better at it than I am at debating and things.
Dee is in a debating team. Sometimes I help her
write her talks. She speaks like an actor, without
any mistakes.

Anyway, have a good Christmas. St. Nicholas
comes to us tomorrow night. We have Santa Claus
too!

I'm sending you more seeds for Christmas.

Love from

Anke

P.S. Give Digger a pat from me.

1 March 1987

Dear Freddie,
You didn't answer my last letter. I forgot to send
the seeds, so here they are now. Our Christmas went

wrong, somehow. Mammie kept saying it wasn't like old Christmasses in The Hague. She talked Dutch all day and this made Beatrix mad, and I didn't know which language to use, so I didn't speak most of the time.

Beatrix came on her own because Whizz has gone to Queensland. I don't think he's going to come back. He's going to be a writer now. Beatrix wants to go up there and she and Mammie have terrible fights because Mammie says Beatrix will end up on the dole. Beatrix says there are waitress jobs up there, but Mammie says we didn't come to Australia for Beatrix to be a waitress. Then Beatrix says what's the difference between a waitress and a shop assistant and Mammie says she didn't bring Beatrix here to be a shop assistant either. I don't know what she'd say if I said I wanted to be a writer. I don't think I've got the courage.

I'm sorry I'm telling you so much about us.

Love from

Anke

1 May 1987

Dear Anke,

I guess you have more to talk about than me. You write better than I do, but you seem to forget an awful lot. Since I last wrote, Digger has gone. It's lonely without him, but I guess that's the way it has to be. For a while he kept coming back, just hanging around the place to say hello. He snuffled and grunted all over us. Dad said, "No biscuits or we'll have him for life." I gave him one anyway. Couldn't say no to those eyes. Digger got that look on his face like he was sorry he was asking, like he knew he should be out in the bush by now. After a while, we didn't see him for a week or so, and now it's a month since he's been.

When I come home from school, the house has that bare feel about it, like even the cupboards are empty. Dad says, "That's life," but he says that about everything.

Love

Freddie

9 *June 1987*

Dear Freddie,
Pappie says I'd forget my head if it wasn't screwed on. Then he says forgetting is no excuse, because I don't forget things I don't want to forget. Something worries me about that, because I wouldn't want to forget my head, would I! And I don't *mean* to forget—it's just that sometimes my head is full of other things.

You must really miss Digger. It's like Beatrix, I suppose. Now she's gone to Queensland. Mammie says we never should have come to Australia. Pappie says if we lived in The Netherlands, Beatrix would be in Amsterdam by now, so what's the difference! What am I supposed to say? But one thing Mammie is happy about—Whizz won't be here when Dee comes around. How big are the first lot of trees now? How much of your farm is trees? You never told me what year you were in. Why don't you answer my questions?

Love from
Anke

21 July 1987

Dear Anke,
1. The first lot of trees are about 10 meters tall.
2. We've got 50 acres of trees and 60 acres of scrub and 150 acres of average-to-rotten paddocks.
3. I am in Year 9.
   You ask a lot of questions.

Love

Freddie

29 August 1987

Dear Freddie,
I hope you are well. I am. It's all right if you don't want to write any more. I was just hoping you'd tell me how things were going.

Love from

Anke

28 September 1987

Dear Anke,
No worries—I've been laid up. Had an accident on the tractor when I was plowing up new land for trees. I had 17 stitches in my leg. It got infected and I had to go to hospital in Bundy. I was there for nine days and Dad drove in every day. I'd just put new seedlings into tubes and I don't think he looked at them the whole time I was gone. Bad luck, eh? The whole lot dead as last night's chops. When I got home, I was on crutches for a week. I was missing Digger, so I went off looking for him. I didn't find him. Hope he's OK out there and found a mate or something.

The other day, Dad bought some sheep for one of the paddocks, even though there isn't much feed. They're eating the weeds, so that's something. Still, I keep thinking of all those dead tubes. Sometimes I hate this place like my mother hated it.

Love

Freddie

7 October 1987

Dear Freddie,
I'm sorry about your leg—you should have told me about it earlier.

Guess what? Next weekend we're going for a picnic to see the tulips in the hills. Pappie worries because Mammie is so quiet, so he said we're going on a "do-dat." I'm scared Mammie will cry heaps, with all those tulips.

I'm sorry about the tubes too, after all your work. I'll send more seeds if you want them.

Love from

Anke

20 October 1987

Dear Anke,
I'll give it one more go.

Love

Freddie

2 November 1987

Dear Freddie,
A terrible thing has happened. Pappie went to pick up Mammie after work. He went to surprise her. When he got out of the car outside the factory, a truck started off backwards and knocked him over. He died next day.

This was three weeks ago, the day before we were going on our picnic to see the tulips. Pappie had planned a special weekend. Mammie still cries every day and hasn't bought your seeds yet.

I don't know what we'll do now. Mammie doesn't want to talk about anything. I remember so many things, but Mammie will not speak about him. Beatrix came home for a week and then went again. Aunt Toos and other people in The Netherlands keep writing letters saying: "Come back home." Our house is quiet, and every afternoon we look at the clock and Pappie doesn't come.

Love from

Anke

25 November 1987

Dear Anke,
I'm sorry about your father. Here is some blossom from
a late wattle that grows under the trees.

With love from

Freddie

6 December 1987

Dear Freddie,
Thank you for the flower. I use it for a bookmark.
Mammie is going to get your seeds soon, because
she is back at work now. She told me last night:
"Pappie came here for us, so we will stay." All the
time we've been here, she has wanted to go back to
Holland. Now, she's going to stay. I'm glad. I was
scared of talking Dutch and walking on cobbles. Still,
this will be a terrible Christmas.

Love from

Anke

21 December 1987

Dear Anke,
Dad reckons Christmas is pretty ratshit too, but it doesn't last that long. You'll be right.

Love

Freddie

5 January 1988

Dear Freddie,
This weekend, Dee came to stay. My room isn't big like hers, that's why I didn't ask her before, but Dee said she liked my room *because* it was small. Mammie made baby pancakes, the first time for ages. We call them "poffies" in our house.

But an awful thing has happened. Dee is going to boarding school. She doesn't want to go, either. I can't think about school without her. Dee is my best friend. Her gran says it won't be so bad, because Dee will be home some weekends and we can do the same things we've always done together. But it will seem a very long time between weekends.

Love
Anke

23 January 1988

Dear Anke,

Thanks for the extra seed you sent. I've started over again—again! The trees on the hill are around ten meters tall now. Here is a photo of me beside the biggest one.

Love

Freddie

30 January 1988

Dear Freddie,
Mammie and I got a real surprise because we thought you'd have black hair and it's red. I like red hair. Dee saw the photo and asked a lot of questions about you. These holidays we have done most things together.

I can't get rid of the feeling that Pappie is in our house. Still, I know now that Mammie and I are going to be friends. Her English is getting better, but sometimes I talk Dutch to her in the evenings. I wish Beatrix would come home. Mammie has only got me now.

Love from
Anke

3 February 1988

Dear Anke,
I hate red hair myself. Now I suppose you'll tell me you've got red hair too. Could you send me a photo one day?

Love

Freddie

11 February 1988

Dear Freddie,
Dee has gone to boarding school. When I said good-
bye, she was very quiet. It was terrible. She had a
big suitcase and a blue and brown uniform and it
was like when people go on a long journey. Her
gran said it was only an hour's drive in the car. Still,
I felt empty inside. I came home and didn't know
what to do. I read a book all day. I told Mammie I
wished I could go to boarding school too and she
went all white and funny. I won't talk about it again.
Anyway, I don't really want to go.

Love from
Anke

20 February 1988

Dear Anke,

I wish I could go to boarding school—get away from this place and play cricket and footie all the time.

Last week Mum sent a parcel for my birthday—eight months late. I didn't open it for a couple of days. Then I thought that she'd gone to all that trouble, so it was pretty rotten of me not to even look at it. Do you know what it was? A book on the Northern Territory! She could have sent a shirt or something. Come to think of it, she wouldn't know the size. Doesn't know the size of her own son. There was no letter, just a note: "With love from Mum." Dad says it shows she thought of me, but that doesn't mean she likes me. I think of her too. I think of lots of people I don't like—like Patrick O'Hara. Sometimes you think more about them than other people. They sort of nag at your brain.

All this has made me decide to write and say: "Thanks for the book," and then forget her.

I'll start thinking about the people I like.

From today.

Love

Freddie

P.S. What about the photograph?

26 February 1988

Dear Freddie,
Once I didn't like this girl called Greta. She put on a funny voice every time she saw me. Then after a while I stopped not liking her, because it made me feel terrible and didn't worry her at all. We're friends now, in a kind of way. Dee rang yesterday afternoon. I told her not to ring, but she did. She hates boarding school . . . I'm glad she hates it. She's coming home tomorrow for almost two whole days.

Love from
Anke

15 March 1988

Dear Anke,
Yesterday I thought Dad had been bitten by a snake.
He'd found clover in the paddock where sheep have
eaten the weeds! He jumped in the air and yelled and
ran around like a nutter. Looks like we've got a good
paddock there. About time. Have you got clover in your
garden?

Love

Freddie

26 March 1988

Dear Freddie,
That's about the first question you've asked me. Our house only has plants in pots, but there's a tree outside the gate that Pappie said was a birch, like the ones in the woods in The Netherlands.

Dee came home for her first weekend. We were going to the movies, but we talked so much that we were too late to get there. Dee said that at school they have all the beds in one long room called a dorm and little rooms called cubicles, where they get dressed. She shares with a skinny girl called Margie, who doesn't wash every day and a fat girl called Val, but they call her Valium because she's a slow-acting dope. (I suppose you've heard that one before?)

Dee's gran is going to ask me to stay a night when Dee comes home for Easter. Just a few days to wait— it seems a long time, but not as long as waiting for trees to grow.

Love from
Anke

12 April 1988

Dear Anke,

Today I found out I'd been calling this bogan Jono Parker by the wrong name. How am I supposed to know everything? He's only in Year 8. We call him Jon O. P. because of all the Johns around the place. He brings his mother along for Open Day and I go: "Hello, Mrs. O'Parker." Everyone rolls around wetting themselves and I get the message I've said the wrong thing. "Parker," says Dad, because he's known them around the joint for years. "It's Mrs. Parker." I feel pretty small, and then that prize prick Patrick O'Hara slides up and goes: "And this is *my* Mum, Mrs. Hara." They all roll around again, so I step forward and give Patrick one on the nose. The little prick lands in the dirt. He looks up with blood all over his dial and his mother is screaming and Dad is saying "Sorry, sorry" all the time and Miss Ritter is glaring at me and pointing to the classroom. On the way there, she goes: "That was uncalled for, Frederick. You must learn to control your temper." Dad calls it talking with my fists. It's a whole lot easier than thinking what to say.

Love

Freddie

P.S. Still no photo.

23 April 1988

Dear Freddie,

Dee didn't come home for Easter. She went to a farm with a friend from her school. We were going to do so many things together. Mammie asked Greta Schiller around on the Saturday. She laughs and tells jokes all the time, but I don't talk to her the way I talk to Dee. I didn't see Greta again after Saturday.

As soon as Dee's gran told me Dee had not come home, I felt so terrible that I wanted to write and tell you. But I've waited until now.

Mammie laughed when I told her about your fight with Patrick O'Hara. Still, I hope you never talk to me with your fists.

Love from

Anke

P.S. Here is a photograph of me in my school uniform.

21 May 1988

Dear Anke,

Thanks for the photo. I'm really glad you haven't got red hair.

While I was out on the western hill this morning, Dad came up to me and said how would I like a new pair of jeans. He said it like he says "Pass the Vegemite" or "Take off your boots." He said he was going into Bundy to get himself a decent pair of trousers and did I want to go too? Poor old Dad. He's never bought a decent pair of trousers in his life. I said why did he want them, and he looked up and down at his old duds, like he'd never seen them before and sort of laughed. It's worth something, to hear Dad laugh. He never roars or anything, but he doesn't laugh much either. Sometimes it shits me off, because he's so bloody boring. He said: "Come on, kid, I sold some sheep yesterday. We're gunna get something for ourselves." I guess it's another late birthday present for me—that's the way Dad would do it, sort of offhand, like he's not really giving you anything.

So now we've both got new trousers and nowhere to go.

Love

Freddie

12 June 1988

Dear Freddie,

Dee's gran told me Dee would be home this weekend, so I went around straight after piano yesterday
morning. Dee opened the door and another girl was
standing beside her. They held the door open and
looked at me and I didn't know what to say. I couldn't
say anything. Then Dee said: "Hello, Anke, this is
Georgia." And Georgia stared at me as if I'd come
to the wrong house, and it did seem like the wrong
house, not a bit like the place I knew. I heard her
gran call out: "Is that you, Anke? Come along in,"
and then Dee and Georgia stood aside and let me
through the door.

I think I asked what they were doing. Dee said
they were playing a new game, but she didn't tell
me what it was. I followed them upstairs to her room
and they had cards spread on the carpet. They sat
down and kept on playing. Dee said Georgia lived
in the country.

"On a farm?" I asked.

Georgia nodded. "Sheep."

I guess that's where Dee went for Easter. I asked
if they had lots of trees. Georgia raised her eye-
brows, as if it were a dumb question. I felt terrible.

Dee said: "She means do you plant trees or are
they there already."

"Oh, we've got masses." She had this posh voice.
I didn't want to tell her about our trees.

They went on playing. I said Mammie would be
wanting me at home, even though she was at work.
When I was already out the door, I heard Dee call
out "Good-bye."

I came home and read a book.

Have you worn your new jeans yet?

Love from

Anke

25 June 1988

Dear Anke,
I wouldn't have anything to do with that Dee. I bet she
and Patrick O'Hara would be an item.

The trees are fine. I've got your photo on the table in
my room. One day I'd like a smiling one.

Love

Freddie

11 July 1988

Dear Freddie,
In my last letter, I think I called your trees *our* trees.
I'm sorry. I didn't mean it. There isn't much happening around here, it's terrible, so I've been reading lots of books and getting ideas for stories. That's what I want to do, write stories.

Next term our school is having dancing classes. I'm not going this year. You don't have to go if you don't want to. If you went to my school, do you think you'd dance with me?

Love
Anke

25 July 1988

Dear Anke,
I don't go much on dancing myself. They don't have classes at our school. When Mum was here, she and Dad sometimes went to the CWA hall on Show Day and I had to go too. Once I went to sleep behind the pie warmer and nobody could find me. After Mum shot through, we didn't go any more until last year. Dad

said he needed a bit of cheering up, so we went in again, just like before. Nothing was different. I sat around the edge with the kids and things, and Dad jigged about with Mrs. Raddici, that blob from the store. It was all a bore. The next weekend, Mrs. Raddici turned up with a jar of that Piccadilly stuff you put on cold lamb. Gross, like I knew it would be.

Guess what. Digger turned up again the other day. Dad and I were sitting down to eat our chops and there was this banging on the kitchen door. He came in like he owned the place and looked in all the cupboards. We said sorry, we had no biscuits, so I gave him a plate of muesli. He shot through without saying thank you, but I reckon he'll be back.

Love

Freddie

4 August 1988

Dear Freddie,

I just opened a package from Beatrix. It's a T-shirt
with a label called Whizzard. Beatrix is working at
Rainbow Beach with Whizz, selling T-shirts and
earrings. Everything they make has a rainbow on it—
the earrings are rainbow-shaped too, only upside
down. I don't know if they make any money, but
it's a good idea, don't you think?

I wish Mammie and I could go up and see them.
We never go anywhere.

Love

Anke

P.S. It's piccalilli. I don't like it either.

21 September 1988

Dear Anke,

Mum sent us an invitation to her wedding in Darwin. I wonder how she thought we were going to get there— if we wanted to go. Azif! That's really the end of things, I guess. The guy's got two kids, so now she's a stepmother. Makes you wonder, doesn't it?

Funny how word gets around, even here in the bush. When Dad and I were in Bundy last week, Patrick O'Hara sleazed around and said: "Hear you've got a stepfather, Forth." Until then, it hadn't hit me that I had a stepfather. I tried not to show it, though. I don't want any stepfather—it's an insult to a good Dad. Dad doesn't say bad things like I feel, but then it's nothing to him. How about that? She's still my mother, so I get the guy as part of the package. They're nothing to Dad. He's got less and I've got more. Work that one out. Guess I'll never see them, anyhow. Why would I want to?

Love

Freddie

6 October 1988

Dear Freddie,
One day you might find that your stepfather is a sort of friend. I'd like someone like that to talk to, even though I can't get Pappie out of my mind. Other times, I try and try and I can't picture him at all. I'm scared it will disappear altogether. It isn't fair that people can go from our minds like that, because if I don't hold him in there, who else will?

Your family and mine are so far away from us. You and I live closer to each other than they do, yet we've never met. Some of the kids at school think this is really weird.

I want to tell you that I saw Dee today. The bus for our Bio. excursion went past her school. I saw her standing on the footpath near the crossing. Our bus pulled up at the lights. She looked up—I think she knew it was our school bus and she was looking for me. I waved and shouted, but it was terrible—the windows were shut and she couldn't hear. Then a girl with a film-star face came running from behind and wrapped her hands around Dee's eyes. Dee spun around, laughing, and forgot about me. They turned and walked towards the school gates with their heads together, talking and giggling. The bus started up and then I couldn't see them any more.

Love

Anke

15 October 1988

Dear Anke,
Mrs. Raddici came across again last weekend and when she saw the trees she said I could get a job anywhere, with my green fingers. And I said: "I'm not going anywhere, now I've got all this going." Dad looked as if I had a roo loose in the top paddock and I think I have, because getting away from here was all I ever wanted. So now I reckon I'm crazy as well as thick. What do you reckon?

Love

Freddie

1 November 1988

Dear Freddie,
Don't ask stupid questions. Sometimes you make me
cross.

Love from
Anke

10 February 1989

Dear Anke,

I haven't written for a while, seeing you think I'm stupid.

I had another fight with Patrick O'Hara yesterday. He's ranting on about lovers and things and when he sees me coming, he says in a loud voice: ". . . now she's made it legit." I give him a filthy glare and he goes, smug as shit: "Why should I be talking about *your* mother? We've all forgotten what she looks like."

I give him a good one on the jaw. He leaps up and butts me in the ribs. So I bash him on the skull. I belt the guts out of him. Like always, it's me that gets the blame. Cunning skunk, O'Hara. Trouble is, he's right. I *have* forgotten what my mother looks like. And I'm not like you—I don't try to remember.

I don't know why I'm telling you all this, except you'd better know what a bastard I am, as well as stupid.

Love

Freddie

1 March 1989

Dear Freddie,
I only mean you're stupid to *say* you're stupid, so will you please not talk like that again.

Our school is having a short story competition called the A. W. Stonehaven Memorial Prize. It's a shield and $50 worth of books. I've heard kids saying I'll win it. I haven't ever won anything in my life. Think of it. Pappie would have been proud—I can just see all the letters he'd write back to The Netherlands. Wow! I *am* getting carried away. I don't really expect to win. But I'll try. This one won't be for Mammie's sake. It'll be for me.

Love from
Anke

P.S. I don't think I like Patrick O'Hara either.

15 April 1989

Dear Anke,
OK then, quits.

Not much is happening around the place, really, but one good thing—I quit school before Easter. Dad can do with a hand now the farm is producing a bit. I'm keeping on with seed trays and tubes. It goes on and on. I get a bit bored with them, but I want to cover the eastern hill by next Christmas. I reckon we've planted close to 10,000 now and we've got a long way to go yet. Dad has to live another 40 years to see them up there, 60 or 70 meters tall. Some nights he's so buggered he says five or six will do—years, I mean. By then, we'll be thinning out to make fence-posts. With good fences, we can keep out the sheep and have more paddocks for nuts. Dad's got ideas about pistachios.

Love

Freddie

30 April 1989

Dear Freddie,
Growing trees sounds like a terrible lot of work to me. I've never sprouted anything, except a carrot top, and then it went all smelly. I'm sowing words instead. I've been reading heaps and getting ideas for stories.

We've got a new girl at school called Maggie Reith, who's moved here from Perth. She's really humongous, with a booming voice that makes everyone cover their ears. She's got hair the color of a copper kettle and bumps on her shins from hockey sticks.

As soon as she heard my name, Maggie said: "Hiya, Tishoo." When everyone stared, she said: "That'll have to do, because I've dropped me 'Ankie." Now she calls me Tishoo all the time. I don't mind except in the mornings when she yells out across the yard: "Ah, Tishoo!" She always talks as if she's yelling to someone across a beach or paddock. All that space over there must make people talk in loud voices. Nobody likes her much and I guess she is a bit bossy. She's already captain of the debating team. Richard Stinson looks daggers every time she opens her mouth. I wish I had the courage to get up and talk like

them. It's all in my head, but I can't bring myself
to do it.

Love from

Anke

15 May 1989

Dear Anke,
If you talk like your letters, *you'd* be captain of the de-
bating team. I don't talk much myself, write even less.
I'm only good at planting trees.

Dad sold more sheep last week and got a good price.
He's opening up another two paddocks and bought 100
more ewes. In one paddock, he's going to plant chest-
nut trees.

I'll be seventeen on Saturday 17 June, and Dad says
seeing you never go anywhere and seeing he's sold some
sheep, would you and your mother like to come and
see the trees? We could pick you up from the train at
Bundy and Dad has made the room nice.

Love

Freddie

28 May 1989

Dear Freddie,

Mammie and I would like to come to see the trees, but Mammie has to work that Saturday. One good thing has happened, though. Mr. Bundred told me that my story is one of the finalists in the Stonehaven Prize. They're going to announce the winner at assembly on 14 July. It sounds like the Academy Awards ". . . and the winner is . . ." My stomach has butterflies already.

I'm really sorry that we can't come to your farm, but thank you for inviting us.

Love from

Anke

1 July 1989

Dear Anke,

We're sorry you couldn't come. Sounds a feeble excuse to me. We thought you'd like to see the trees. From Bundy it's only 20 minutes' drive to Weatherly.

I didn't have much of a birthday. Nothing from Mum again. And Patrick O'Hara got best on ground at the district lightning premiership.

Love

Freddie

14 July 1989

Dear Freddie,
I'm home here by myself. I don't know how to write about this morning. Before assembly, Mr. Bundred called me into the study and gave me my story. He said the judges would make their decision after the final three stories had been read at assembly. My heart crashed down somewhere near my shoes—it was as if it had stopped beating altogether. Then it started thumping inside my head and I wanted to bolt out of the building. I held the pages in both hands and stared at them. Mr. Bundred said: "I'll call each of you to read in turn," and opened the door to see me out. I knew I couldn't do it. I walked from the room and later I found myself in the schoolyard, standing in the middle of the bitumen, and kids were laughing. I was staring at the pages and they looked like something I'd never seen before. I don't know who won the competition. It wasn't me. Now I look at my story and it's mine again, but what for? Look, I'm sorry this is all about me. I really am. And I *do* want to come to Weatherly—it's just not easy for us to come. It's not easy for me to explain, either. I can usually say anything when I write, but not this time.

It's been a bad week. On Monday, Maggie brought all these cakes to school. She keeps asking people home to eat her Mum's cakes and nobody wants to go. But Mrs. Reith goes on making them. So Maggie brought this huge box to school, for everyone to have one. They were butterfly cakes with cream in the middle and icing sugar dusted on the wings. Some of the kids looked in the box and said: "Couldn't you get rid of them on anyone else?"

I took another to make Maggie think I liked them. Well, I did quite like them. Maggie looked pleased, so I ate four. I felt sick all afternoon. I couldn't eat any dinner at night and I didn't get my maths done, but I had to say I forgot to do it, so Maggie wouldn't know the cakes had made me sick. So then I had to stay in after school and write stupid lines—"I must not forget to do my homework"—which did me no good at all, because I hadn't forgotten this time. I felt *so* mad.

I'm on my own tonight, because Mammie is working. All the form except me has gone to dancing class. I heard the music when I was coming home from piano last week and I thought maybe I will go next year, perhaps. I'm glad dancing is on Fridays. They talk about it all weekend and by Monday they've mostly run out of steam. While they're dancing, I'm sitting here writing. Do you think I'm stupid?

Love from

Anke

4 August 1989

Dear Anke,
Another question! But I've got one too—*when* are you coming to Weatherly?

Love

Freddie

19 August 1989

Dear Freddie,
Please keep asking and one day we will come.

Love from

Anke

1 September 1989

Dear Anke,
Good. I'll telephone you soon, to talk you into it.

Love

Freddie

12 September 1989

Dear Freddie,
No, don't telephone. I'll let you know. Perhaps we'll come for your birthday next year.

Love from

Anke

5 October 1989

Dear Anke,

I'm not *that* thick and I can tell when you're putting me off. It's a long time till my birthday next year. I wouldn't mind getting away from this place for Christmas, but it's the worst time for us to leave. I'm getting a bit jack of the place.

Love

Freddie

15 November 1989

Dear Freddie,

Maggie came around and asked me to go wind-surfing. I said I couldn't do it, but she said she'd teach me. Help! Maggie's parents bought a house near the port, so Maggie and her little brother could keep on wind-surfing. In Perth they used to sail across the river and stop off at their Aunty Jo's for afternoon tea. If you tried that on the bay here, you might end up in Bass Strait. Maggie says that's OK—she could handle that—but she doesn't know a single person on the other side who'd give her a cola. Neither do I. Maggie says this is a good thing to do in a new place, because wherever you are, while you're out sailing you're on your own. You don't have to talk to anyone. That's one reason I like it.

It was terrible at first. Terrible! Maggie kept screaming out: "Ah—Tishoo! Straighten your arms!" Then she'd yell out: "Hopeless!" But after a few times I got the hang of it. *Hang* is the right word too.

Maggie is a good friend, even if I do have to eat too many of Mrs. Reith's cakes.

Everything is all right at home and sometimes to

please Mammie I talk to her in Dutch when she comes home from work.

Love from
Anke

20 December 1989

Dear Anke,
Now you'll never want to come to Weatherly. Don't blame you, really. A couple of weeks ago, I managed to get down to Gran's for a few days. Sale leaves this place for dead. I reckon I could talk Dad into letting me get a job down there some time. We could do with the extra money and I could do with a bit more action. Right now though, Dad needs an extra hand to get the place going. That's me, a cheap hand.

One thing I've noticed—you say terrible a terrible lot. I bet you were never terrible at anything.

Love
Freddie

4 February 1990

Dear Freddie,

How terrible, terrible, terrible! There, I've written it for the last time. I hadn't noticed that I wrote it all the time. I don't say it, *ever,* so there.

Mammie knows now that I want to be a writer. She doesn't say much about it, but she knows for sure that I'll never make a doctor. A lot of things have changed since we came to Australia. Nothing has worked out the way they planned.

Last time we heard from Beatrix, Whizz had gone to Bali and she was down on the Gold Coast, getting drowned in rain that she said never happened there. She was thinking of heading for Cairns—there's a commune up in the mountains somewhere. When Mammie reads Beatrix's postcards, she goes all deadly pale and I talk in Dutch like mad until she gets over the latest shock. Last week, Mammie said: "Your Dutch is improving, Anke," and we both laughed and laughed.

I can't describe how it feels now I can manage Maggie's sailboard. The holidays flew. The other day I sailed out to the center of the bay and people waved to me from a container ship. Out there, I felt really me, freer than ever before.

Our school has invited a school from South Aus-

tralia to come across in the winter holidays for a
series of debates. There will be lots of things organized besides debates, so those holidays will pass as
quickly as the last ones did.

Love from

Anke

18 March 1990

Dear Anke,
At least *you're* not bored out of your mind. Here, it's the same old slog every day. One thing happened, though, since I last wrote. Dad and I went across to O'Haras to look at a ram. Patrick came simpering out of the house like a car salesman. I suppose they needed our money to put up their posh curtains. You should see their house. You'd think they lived in Toorak or somewhere instead of the backblocks of Bundy. If you ask me, there's something fishy about the O'Haras. Anyway, Dad reckoned it was a good ram and Mr. O'Hara said it was insured and Patrick sleazed and squirmed until I could hardly keep my breakfast down, but I never said: "O'Hara, you make me want to throw up," because Dad really wanted that ram.

He—the ram—is keeping the ewes happy, and maybe when we have lambs playing around the place we'll get you to Weatherly.

Love

Freddie

10 April 1990

Dear Freddie,
I've been helping with plans for the debating trip.
Three teams from Centervale High, South Australia,
are coming for a week in July. We're having a bus
trip to the snow and a day in the art gallery and a
party in the gym on the last night. Today, I've been
making streamers for the party. We had rolls of pa-
per everywhere, all blue and yellow, and we've bought
hundreds of balloons already. All the time we're
twisting and cutting, we're working out what to say
in the debates. Maggie keeps saying: "Whadaya-
reckon, Tishoo?" I'm the brains of the outfit, because I put half the speeches together for them. I'm
glad I don't have to get up and do the talking.

I hope this letter isn't boring you. Sometimes I
feel as if I'm writing about me and you're writing
about you and we're not talking to each other, so
please tell me more about your Dad and how the
sheep are going and especially the trees—and you.

Love from
Anke

25 May 1990

Dear Anke,
If you want to know all these things, then why don't you come and find out? You know it's my birthday again soon.

Love

Freddie

4 June 1990

Dear Freddie,
It's a bit late now for us to come for your birthday
and then we have the debates. I know this sounds
silly, when there are so many weekends in a year.
But you never come to the city, do you?

Everything is go go go at school. Richard Stinson
is going around with the biggest head you've ever
seen—he thinks he'll be PM one day. But he did
thank me for an idea I gave him for "The Pen Is
Mightier Than the Sword" (affirmative). It came to
me when I was thinking of you and me and our
letters. I think I'd win in the end, because I can pull
things apart with words and then put them back
together again. You can't do that with your fists,
can you? With a pen, you can do anything.

Love from

Anke

15 June 1990

Dear Freddie,
The Head said today that if you weren't in a debating team, you couldn't go to any of the things they've organized for the holidays. I didn't say a word when I heard. Everyone looked at me, though. Maggie stuck up for me and so did Richard Stinson. They said I'd done half the work. I'd even offered to have one of the Centervale kids to stay, but they paired them off with debaters. Maggie said someone here might get sick and I could offer again, but I don't feel like it now. I've never been to the snow, have you?

Love from
Anke

23 June 1990

Dear Anke,
Come up here instead. There's no snow or art galleries or smart talkers, but a few things are worth seeing I suppose. I could pick you and your mother up from the train—I'm a legit driver now (I've only been driving around Weatherly for ten years!).

Just let us know what day you could come.

Love
Freddie

18 July 1990

Dear Freddie,
Everything was all right while we were writing letters, but we should never have met.

Now you know why we took so long to come. Imagine how I felt, stepping off the train at the station. I knew I wouldn't be able to get the words out.

I felt bad that I hadn't told you. I wasn't trying to deceive you, truly. It was just that in the beginning it wasn't important, and then it was so good having someone to write to, I just couldn't do it. Your letters were the nicest thing that ever happened to me—and I was scared you'd stop writing or that you'd be mad with me. Perhaps I *was* deceiving you, hiding behind the pages. It was easy for me to write.

I know you might never want to see me again. I understand. Really I do. But I hope you'll keep writing and telling me about the trees. You're a real Mr. Sprouts. Mammie and I loved those trees and can't imagine what Weatherly was like without them. I've never been in a place like that before—it speaks to you, doesn't it? While we were there, we didn't have to talk. It was the nicest place I've ever been.

Love from

Anke

30 July 1990

Dear Anke,
What a lot of bloody rot! I don't know what you're going on about. I'm no talker myself, you know, so a stutter is nothing to me. It's the yackers I can't hack.

I was hoping you'd say you liked it here and I really thought you did. Dad was rapt to think you liked it. You were our first real visitors. He says that if your mother will let you, you can come again on your own. I hope you will. And I'd still like a smiling photo, so there.

Love

Freddie

9 August 1990

Dear Freddie,

You *do* want to see me again! Next time I won't be afraid to come. I felt comfortable with you. You didn't hurry me along or step in before I'd got the words out. You've got no idea how some of the kids torment me. They turn around in class and hiss: "Spit it out! Spit it out!" That's why I never put my hand up, even when I know the answer. Last term I said I had a sore throat when we had to read, but the teacher said she'd heard that one before.

The debaters had a great time with the South Australian kids. Thanks to you, I didn't mind so much that I missed out on it all.

Tonight, Mammie has gone out with a friend. Everything is better since we came to Weatherly.

Love from

Anke

20 August 1990

Dear Anke,

I tried to get Dad to put some sheep in the Royal Show. I thought it might get us to town for a change, but we'd missed the closing date by yonks. It put the idea into Dad's head, though, and he says he'll have a crack at the Bundy show in March.

What I really wanted was to get to the footie, of course. I've never been to a finals match . . . as if I'd get a ticket! And I'd come to see you. What do you reckon? Suppose I'll have to wait another year.

Love

Freddie

30 August 1990

Dear Freddie,
Guess who came to see us on Sunday afternoon? Dee's gran. She brought some daffodils from her garden. Mammie gave me a filthy look when I started to say I liked wattle and things like that.

Dee has gone to school in Switzerland and then she's going to live with her father in America. I don't suppose I'll ever see her again. Do you know that before she went to Geneva, she spent two weeks at a schoolfriend's place in The Hague? So, in the end, Dee got to The Netherlands before I did.

I can tell Dee's gran misses her a lot. Before, she could have been someone's mother, but now she really looks like a gran. I told her I'd visit her like I did before, even though Dee won't be there. It will be good to have someone to talk to.

Love from

Anke

12 September 1990

Dear Anke,

It's good that you've got Dee's gran. Grans are OK, even if they do kick you out of your bedroom.

Dad's been going into Bundy a bit lately. He's easier to get along with now I'm around to do the hard slog. Last Wednesday he brought home a pizza and all these packs of Chinese chow. We didn't have chops for three days. He'd never had a pizza before . . . said he reckoned he could get a taste for the Iti—without anchovies.

Love

Freddie

20 September 1990

Dear Freddie,

I wish I could send you a pizza from the shop around the corner. They're my *favorite* food, without anchovies or garlic. Whenever I eat garlic, I feel terrible all night. Terrible—and this time I mean it. Now I can tell you why I used to write it all the time— because it's one word I can't say. It just won't come out. It's the most terrible word.

Mammie says it's all in my head, because that's what people always told her. Did you see the string of purple beads around her neck? Her great aunt made her wear them when she was a little girl—she said they helped to cure a stutter. Mammie doesn't believe it, but she believes it enough not to stop wearing them. Mammie still stutters sometimes, but not like me. It was easier for her when she was a girl— everyone spoke the same language in their house.

Whenever anyone said I should have treatment, Mammie went tight-lipped and grim, because she'd been sent to a psychiatrist. She didn't want that to happen to me. But there are speech pathology clinics near here and since we came to Weatherly I think that I could try that.

Things have been pretty quiet down here. I've been writing and writing. Words come from my fingers more smoothly than from my lips, so I'm happy to be here alone. But yesterday morning the sun was shining and Maggie came banging on the door: "Hey, Tishoo, come wind-surfing." So I did.

I hadn't forgotten how to do it. I used her brother's board and we got sunburnt faces and rumbling stomachs because we stayed out nearly all day. So today I'm limping around the house and Maggie is out there again, whizzing across the bay. All I need tonight is a good pizza, without anchovies or garlic.

How are things at Weatherly? I'd really like to help with the trees one day.

Love from

Anke

29 September 1990

Dear Anke,
I'll be planting out seedlings in the next three weeks, if
you want to help. Dad thinks it's a great idea because
he's busy with the sheep. Will your mother let you come?

Love
Freddie

12 October 1990

Dear Freddie,
Everything is different after the last few days. Nobody has ever wanted to touch me till now. I go over and over the last evening in my mind and each time it is newer than before. When we came in from the dark, the kitchen was bright and your voice was loud and my face was red and my hands were shaking. Everything in the kitchen looked different from just an hour before. Your father smiled and said: "Have a cuppa," and the clatter of his spoon in the mug sounded like a gong ringing in my ears. I like your father. He didn't say a thing. I knew I wouldn't be able to speak.

Dear Mr. Sprouts, I love your farm and the lambs and the place in the trees that your father calls The Cathedral. Your forest is a miracle and I'm happier with you there than I've ever been with anyone, even Pappie.

Love from

Anke

27 October 1990

Dear Anke,

I was waiting at the road box when your letter came. I thought you were never going to write.

It's stinking hot here already and the wind is burning the leaves off the trees. Dad's been clearing mistletoe out of some of the older ones. We don't put it over the door at Christmastime or anything, but if you came we might.

Sometimes I walk up the track to The Cathedral, just to sit there. Nobody except Dad has ever helped with the trees before. It will be good when you come again. The whole place feels better when you're here.

Love

Freddie

9 November 1990

Dear Mr. Sprouts,
The other day, Mammie said: "You look different."
I *feel* different too. And I'm more forgetful than ever.
   If only you were here—in more ways than one. I
could do with your bush sense. I got lost again yesterday, looking for a bookshop. Mammie always tells
me to ask directions, but I like to work it out for
myself. It's easier than asking. Using my "do-dat,"
Pappie used to call it. "Anke, you can do-dat." Well,
this time I couldn't. I walked about three kilometers
in the wrong direction. "If all else fails, read the
instructions," says our computer teacher, so when I
got home I looked up the street directory. I'll have
another go tomorrow. If I know where I'm going
and it's a self-serve, I don't have to speak a single
word to anyone.
   I hope our new trees are settling in after that heat
wave. I want them to become your most special forest. I keep hearing your voice and what you said to
me that night.

Love from
Anke

23 November 1990

Dear Anke,
One day you'll be a famous writer, if you can find your way through the plot. You know I'd rather a prize writer than a prize talker any day.

Dad says hello and when are you coming again. He's getting a taste for having you around the place. Last Wednesday he went into Bundy again and when he came back he'd chucked out his brown check shirt and bought two denim ones. And would-you-believe—moleskins! Pretty neat. If you say you'll come again soon, I might spiff myself up a bit too. Bring your Mum if you want to. I'm a bit behind, planting out a new lot of trees, so why don't you come before Christmas?

Love

Freddie

6 December 1990

Dear Mr. Sprouts,
I've finished my exams. I hope I kept my mind on the job long enough to get into that Professional Writing course. I won't know until January. Most of the kids from our year—except Maggie and me—have gone to Surfers or taken jobs. I should have gone for an interview back in September, but I didn't.

Maggie says we're going wind-surfing later today. Her mother doesn't make so many cakes now and Maggie doesn't shout as loudly—or maybe I've grown used to it. Perhaps everything just seems better to me these days.

I can't wait to come to Weatherly again, but I won't be able to come before Christmas. In the new year, I might have something to show you.

Love from

Anke

11 January 1991

Dear Anke,
I don't know why you couldn't come before Christmas. Don't you want to come or something?

Well, it's too late now. We had a lousy Christmas. That storm wrecked the place. We had no electricity for days. Everything went rotten—and we've lost 1,000 trees. They're piled up like matchsticks in a long line across the hills. A freak wind, that. They say those strip storms only come once in a couple of hundred years. Just our luck.

I won't be planting again.

Love

Freddie

21 January 1991

Dear Freddie,
Why is it too late? Let me come and help you. We can plant again.

I cried when I opened your letter. Mammie said I was crying for myself, but I was crying for you and for the trees. Why didn't you tell me earlier? Please let me come. I'm thinking of you all the time.

Your loving
Anke

4 February 1991

Dear Anke,
Thinking doesn't help anymore. I've done all I'm going to do around here. It's been a waste of bloody time. Dad's cleaning up the house and paddocks. He thinks the trees are my job. Well, he's got another think coming.

You reckon you understand? You couldn't. If you want to understand, then come and take a look at this dump. No, don't. I won't be here. I'm not hanging around for any more disasters. Gran will give me a bed and there could be work going in Sale. At least I'll be away from trees—dirty, rotten, stinking trees.

Love

Freddie

18 February 1991

Dear Freddie,
When I read your letter, I felt I hardly knew you.
Don't let us go back to the beginning again. A
thousand trees is not so many when you've planted
thirty times that number. I'll send more seed.

I have plenty of moments when I can't face things,
but every time some other thing comes along to stir
my interest and immediately there is a future again.
It will be like that for you with the trees.

Please tell me you haven't gone to your grand-
mother's. I had a surprise for you, but it will keep.
Let me come and we can work together.

Your loving

Anke

5 April 1991

Dear Anke,

I've been at Gran's six weeks now. The food's better than at home and there's more life around the joint. I went to a disco at The Rigger last Friday. The girls were a lot better than the ones at Bundy.

Dad manages Weatherly fine without me and you know I've always wanted to live in a city. So, you see, everything's jake.

Love

Freddie

To Freddie,

Happy Birthday

Love Anke

18 July 1991

Dear Anke,
Thanks for the card for my birthday. You didn't write much on it. Is anything wrong?

Love

Freddie

12 August 1991

Dear Freddie,
What do you *think* is wrong? Don't you understand? You're treating me like a stranger.

Love from

Anke

24 September 1991

Dear Anke,
I didn't say I *liked* the other girls, did I? It would be better if you were here. Don't expect me to write mushy stuff all the time—give me a break. For once in my life I can go to the movies and play the pinnies and not get muddy boots the whole damn time.
   Happy birthday for the other day.

Love
Freddie

30 October 1991

Dear Freddie,

All right, I understand—I suppose I do. It just doesn't feel the same as when I was writing to Weatherly. And all year you haven't once asked how my course was going. Well, I'm going to tell you anyway. I'm still a long way from becoming a writer. There are so many people hidden out there pounding away at their word processors that I go through moments when I think the world doesn't need my words as well. Then there are other moments when I sit here for two or three hours and the words pour out, as if someone else was writing them. They come from a mood inside me and speak in a voice I didn't know was mine. It's good to have that voice—it's as if I've been given another me. When this happens, I float to College the next day; the excitement of the words carries me there.

I miss Weatherly, but I really do hope you're happy in Sale.

Love from

Anke

29 November 1991

Dear Anke,
Things are going pretty well here in Sale. About Weatherly—Mrs. Raddici has moved in with Dad. What do you think about that? The minute I go, someone else moves in. Not only that—they started doing the place up and putting on another room. They're welcome to the lot!

They were coming to Gran's for Christmas, but now Dad says he can't leave Weatherly because it's another bad bushfire year. There's no way they'll get me back there, so I guess it's just Gran and me for Christmas.

I've got a casual job in a video shop, but there's work out on the rigs. I might get a job there next year.

You haven't asked how the trees are going. I don't know, of course—*and I don't care.*

See you in town one day, eh?

Love
Freddie

6 December 1991

Dear Freddie,

It's a year since I said I couldn't come to Weatherly before Christmas. You thought I was putting you off again, but it was just the opposite. I wanted to surprise you. I wanted to arrive, talking as well as I can write. I couldn't come before Christmas, because I was doing a full week of therapy—it was a hard week, but it was worth it.

If I'd known what lay ahead, I might have come instead of doing the course. Well, it's done now and I can't surprise you, so I may as well tell you about it.

I did it because of you. Before, when people suggested treatment, I wouldn't listen. I pretended I didn't care, when underneath it was what I wanted most in the world. A bit of a martyr, that was me. Knowing you helped me to face up to things—it's something Mammie has never truly done. Now I know how an alcoholic must feel—you have to admit that you need help.

I went along to this clinic and first I got the bad news. There's no cure for a stutter. "What's the point of all this?" I thought. Then they told me the good news: I need never stutter again. There might not be a cure, but you can be taught another way, a way of getting the words out without stuttering. Imagine how I felt about that! I need never stutter again! I couldn't believe it, after all this time. I wanted to run all the way to Weatherly to tell you. But I wanted to surprise you, too, so I kept it a secret.

The storm ruined everything. Still, I'll tell you what happened at the clinic. I can't believe I waited so long to find I need not have suffered like that. I learned a whole new way of speaking. Smooth speech, they call it, really slow and controlled. For a while I sounded like a robot that was running out of batteries. But I didn't care. I could string words together, then sentence after sentence, without a single block. Sometimes, at home in the evenings, things went wrong again. It's hard to stop and take a deep breath and slow down your speech when you want to tell your mother that the potatoes are boiling over and there's someone at the door. Mammie isn't very patient, either. Listening to someone speaking at 60 syllables a minute isn't easy, I suppose. She kept on butting in all the time.

Towards the end of the week, they made us go to a bank and stutter deliberately to the teller. I felt crazy, but it taught me something. I know now that I can turn it on and off and that, if ever I lose the technique, I can find it again—by myself.

Maggie was a true friend during this time. I rang

her every morning and she listened to my snail talk. I still ring her sometimes, because I feel comfortable with her.

At the end of the week, I felt exhausted and exhilarated at the same time. I was thinking of all the things I could join in at College, but mostly I was waiting until after Christmas, when I could come to Weatherly and surprise you.

It never happened. Don't feel bad about it, because the therapy has changed so many other things for the better.

Sale sounds a pretty good city, if that's what you want. Take care.

Love from

Anke

13 February 1992

Dear Freddie,

Thank you for your telephone call. We had so short a time and I'm sorry I wasted the moments with tears. They were tears of shock—and happiness, to hear your voice.

I thought you were safe in Sale. If I'd known you were there, in the thick of it, I would have been twice as frantic. I sat by the radio all day, hoping Weatherly wasn't burning and that your father was all right (and Mrs. Raddici) and the trees.

You said it was a miracle your house was saved and that the forest went off like a string of grenades. Was anything left?

I'm glad most of the sheep escaped . . . but the trees?

I said I was shocked that you were at Weatherly, but underneath I knew you'd be there.

Love from

Anke

20 February 1992

Dear Anke,

Things are pretty bad, but we're better off than a lot of people. The O'Haras lost everything.

It was all a nightmare and it's not over yet. I heard about the fires the day before. I know those winds. They can flick flames across a river or a six-lane highway in one second flat. I told Gran I had to go to Weatherly. I had to save the trees. She said: "No, stay here, you're safe here." But I had to go.

I went out on the road and hitched a lift almost to Ricketts. This truckie fellow took me all that way. When we got to the top of the ridge, we could see the smoke. He reckoned it was 10 or 15 kilometers away and he wasn't going any further along that road.

"Drop me here," I said. "I'll get there somehow."

"I can't leave you here, mate."

"Leave me. Someone will come." I got out when he stopped to turn around.

"Get back, you idiot," he yelled. But I started running. I half ran, half walked, until I couldn't go another step.

I was sitting on a gravel hump when the CFA truck came past. They were in a real hurry. They stopped in a blast of red dust. "What the hell . . . ?" They pulled me on board. I told them I was going home to save my

114

trees. "You're staying with us," they said. "It's the safest thing we can do with you now."

They belted around corners, heading towards the smoke. I could smell it now. I reckoned it was coming from O'Haras' place. We drove for half an hour, I suppose, and it sure was O'Haras' place. We could see the flames then.

They drove straight through the gate, like it was ice-cream sticks. Up the road and a shortcut across the paddock, but too late, the house was already alight. It was like a tree burning—flames shooting everywhere—only this was a house, that posh house of O'Haras'. The noise was terrible, like a train coming at us full pelt. Geez, I was scared someone was inside that oven. I can't explain how hot it was, like you can't believe it hasn't killed you. Embers were flying off in the wind.

The guys on the truck ran off with their hoses. I wasn't much of a help. I rushed around yelling for the O'Haras. I saw their old ute in the yard and it was a goner. There was another burnt-out truck by the shed. I didn't know then that it was ours.

Then the O'Haras came running from behind the house, all black and greasy-looking from sweat and ashes. They'd been trying to save the animals. There were four people, not three, and I saw that the other one was Dad.

He didn't ask what I was doing there. He just stared at me and lifted his hands in the air, kind of hopeless.

Patrick O'Hara said: "Get in the car, Freddie."

"What do you mean?" I think that's what I said.

"We're going to your place."

His house was a goner and he talked about going to my place! "What about here?" I said.

"There's nothing more we can do right now."

Mr. O'Hara sort of staggered and leaned against one of the CFA guys. He moved an arm towards the car. "Go on, off you go. Be careful, that's all."

Patrick looked me up and down and said: "You've got useless bloody gear on."

"What do you mean?" Geez, I must have cheesed him off.

"That singlet, for God's sake." He opened the boot and threw a roll of clothes at me. "Put them on, idiot."

I pulled on a long-sleeved cotton shirt and a woolen jumper. I don't know how I didn't pass out. Guess I thought we were heading for certain death, anyhow. I did have my heavy boots on and that was my one bit of sense. Otherwise, the O'Haras had thought of everything. In the car they had woolen blankets and bottles of water. They even had tennis balls to block down-pipes. They'd put spares of all these things in the ute, too, but that was one of the first things to go.

Dad got in the front with Patrick and I sat in the back.

It was like a bloody oven. I mean, the temperature outside was around 105°, so I reckon you could cook a
roast inside the car. I hoped I didn't have to get under
a blanket as well—reckon I'd have died with one more
thing on my back.

Patrick drove like crazy, but I wasn't scared. I didn't
think about accidents, then. We got to Weatherly in 15
minutes flat, through all that smoke and dust. Dad didn't
say a thing the whole way. I don't know what I said,
but Patrick said: "When we get there, if your house is
OK, I'll get on the roof and you connect the hoses."

Dad had shut the place up before he went across to
help O'Haras. That was good thinking. Mrs. Raddici was
inside, locked in the bathroom I reckon. She came
screaming to the door: "Get inside, it's safer here."

"I'm going to save the trees."

"The trees will grow again," she said. As if *she* knew.

"I'm going up there."

Dad was running around with a hose and buckets
and Patrick was already on the roof. They filled all the
gutters from the gravity tank and kept on hosing the
place down. You could hear the fire coming. The smoke
was choking us. The flames were licking around the
fences, coming from behind O'Haras and up our western hill.

The CFA truck came roaring in just as I was getting
bags from the shed. Dad and Patrick were still hosing

the roof. Mrs. Raddici came out and threw buckets around. The CFA guys drove me to the forest and we started battering at the edges of the flames. It was pretty futile, I can tell you. A bugger like that wasn't going to stop at a few thrashes with a sack. But we had to do it.

There was a bit of a willy-willy then, and bang, some of the trees went off like rockets. The fire raced up the hill, like it didn't care a damn about anything. I kept praying the eastern hill wouldn't go too. It reached the top of the western hill, like it was eating trees as it went. Then it leaped across Mercers' paddock next door and up their valley. The CFA guys headed off in that direction. I didn't know how long they'd been on the job or how long they could keep going.

I stood there in a sort of daze. The wind had dropped or sort of passed over and the noise had almost stopped—just the odd crack of things falling and shifting back into place, sighing, like they were people only just alive.

I could hardly drag myself back to the house. Dad and Mrs. Raddici had gone inside. I climbed on to the roof and sat there with Patrick and we hardly said a thing. The smoke had cleared and we could see for kilometers—all grey and black with embers glowing like city lights.

We sat there for I don't know how long and watched the sun burn down behind the blackened trees. It was sort of peaceful up there, like after you've had a tooth out. I knew Patrick didn't want to go home.

Later on, Dad went and brought Mr. and Mrs. O'Hara here for the night. They stayed two days, and now they've gone back with a caravan, to clear up and start again. They've got bloody nothing.

While they were here, Patrick helped with the trees. I didn't know where to start. And I don't know if I'll ever finish. It's a lonely job, working with dead trees. Not all the western trees have lost their crowns, though, and the rest have dropped their seed—millions of them— to start over again on their own. Mrs. R. was right (though I'm not telling her) that they'll grow again. We're lucky they were old enough to carry seed. In a funny way, bushfires help them to carry on their family line.

I'll be months working on this western hill. But behind me, most of the eastern hill is green and cool and on still days I can hear the water running through the gully.

I said it was a miracle that our house was saved, but it wasn't really. It was Patrick O'Hara, mostly Patrick's planning and a bit of luck that our ordinary old house had concrete floors and verandahs. The O'Haras' posh place with its fancy deck was a sitting duck to catch the sparks.

One thing that's come out of all this—I've beaten you to write a book! I'll never write another letter like this

one. I haven't even said I'm pleased about the therapy.
A stutter never worried me, you know that.
   But I'm really very pleased.

Love

Freddie

14 March 1992

Dear Freddie,
What can I say, except that I want to come and
help.

Love from

Anke

21 March 1992

Dear Anke,
I could do with a hand—no excuses this time.

Love

Freddie

Circa 2042

A *wind began somewhere in the valley and circled upwards until the leaves above their heads were singing.*

From the hill, they could see a car winding towards the house below them. A man got out and walked to the door. They watched as Rick waved and pointed the man towards the hill. The man started walking.

"Hello, there," he said when he reached the ridge. "Nice place you've got here. Been here long?"

"Fair while, fair while," said Freddie. "But we don't run things anymore. Down there's our son Patrick—he's in charge now."

The man held out his hand. "Montague's the name. We're doing a regional flora survey."

"Frederick Forth." Freddie shook the man's hand. "And this is my wife, Anke Duyker."

"You're Anke Duyker, the writer?"

"Yes. Yes, I am," said Anke in her slow, sure way.

The man peered at her over his glasses, then twisted his neck to squint towards the sky. Clouds spiraled above the treetops. The man blinked, dizzily. "Real giants, aren't they? You were lucky to find a place with a natural forest like this."

Anke looked across at Freddie. He smiled and took her hand. "Sure," he said. "Sure, we were lucky."

Errol Broome

is a newspaper journalist, full-time writer for television and radio, sometime gardener, full-time mother of three, and author of nine books for children. She lives with her husband and youngest son in Melbourne, Australia.

Dear Mr. Sprouts is her first book to be published in the United States.